**D-Day: Battle on the Beach**

# THE RANGER IN TIME SERIES

# D-Day: Battle on the Beach

## KATE MESSNER

**illustrated by**
## KELLEY McMORRIS

**Scholastic Press / New York**

Library of Congress Cataloging-in-Publication Data
Names: Messner, Kate, author. | McMorris, Kelley, illustrator.
Title: D-Day : battle on the beach / Kate Messner ; illustrated by Kelley McMorris.
Description: New York : Scholastic Inc., [2018] | Series: Ranger in time ; 7 | Summary: Ranger, a time-traveling golden retriever with search-and-rescue training, heads to Normandy on the morning of the D-Day invasion where he meets Leo, a Jewish boy who is hiding with a local farmer, and Walt, a young American soldier fighting to free France from the Nazis.
Identifiers: LCCN 2017010030
Subjects: LCSH: World War, 1939-1945 — Campaigns — France — Normandy — Juvenile fiction. | CYAC: World War, 1939-1945 — Campaigns — France — Normandy — Fiction. | Golden retriever — Fiction. | Dogs — Fiction. | Time travel — Fiction. | War — Fiction. | Adventure and adventurers — Fiction.
Classification: LCC PZ10.3.M5635 Dad 2018 | DDC [Fic] — dc23
LC record available at https://lccn.loc.gov/2017010030

ISBN 978-1-338-13393-6

10 9 8 7 6 5 4 3 2 1      18 19 20 21 22

Printed in the United States of America    113
First printing 2018

Book design by Ellen Duda and Maeve Norton

*For Penny Smith and the readers at Hornell Intermediate School*

## Chapter 1

# THE LONGEST NIGHT

"Hold on!"

Walt Burrell clung to the railing of the ship as it rocked on five-foot waves. Three dozen men were packed together on his landing craft. It was one of thousands crossing the English Channel on a mission to free France from the Nazis. The Allied invasion had begun.

Last night, as Walt and the other men boarded the ship, they'd been handed an order of the day from General Eisenhower. "You are about to embark upon the Great Crusade, toward which we have striven these many months," the order read. "The eyes of the world are upon you. The hopes and prayers of liberty-loving people everywhere march with you . . ."

Walt had folded the order and tucked it in a pocket. He'd climbed on board with the other men to begin the longest night of his life.

The sea was stormy and rough. Home seemed a lifetime away. Walt's stomach churned as the ship surged over another wave. He squeezed his eyes shut against the wind and rain and tried to remember his papa's farm in Virginia. For a moment, he could almost smell the rich earth and baking corn bread he'd left behind when he joined the army. He was only sixteen, but he'd lied about his age and enlisted to fight for his country.

Walt's unit, the 320th Barrage Balloon Battalion, had spent months at training camp

in Tennessee. Like many other soldiers, they'd woken up before dawn to go on twenty-five-mile hikes through the woods. They'd run obstacle courses, crawling with their rifles under barbed wire fences. But this unit had a special mission — handling the enormous barrage balloons that would fly over the American troops in France, keeping enemy planes away. Walt and the other men had practiced launching and maneuvering the car-size balloons. The plan was to raise them over the beaches of Normandy, where the balloons would form a sort of defensive curtain in the sky, protecting Allied troops from German planes.

And now it was time.

The night journey across the sea had been dark and murky, but suddenly, the sky lit up in the distance. Searchlights swept the cliffs. The air thundered with the pounding of bombs. Allied forces were trying to knock out German defenses before Walt and the other men came ashore.

"You ready, Big Walt?" his friend Ernest shouted over the waves.

Walt almost smiled at the joke. He was the skinniest man in his battalion. The nickname that had felt so lighthearted at training camp felt different here. Not a single man on the landing craft seemed big enough for what they were about to face on the beaches.

The blasts grew louder and louder as Walt's boat passed the battleships firing at shore. The sky was growing lighter now, even in the clouds and rain. The sea was crowded with smaller landing vessels like the one Walt was in. Waves sloshed over their sides and tossed them about as if they were toys in a bathtub. German machine gun fire blasted over the water.

Walt's heart thudded through his jacket. Would they even make it to land?

Already, two shells had exploded just feet from his boat, sending up great sprays of salt water. The gunfire was almost constant, but the landing craft pushed on toward the beach.

Finally, someone shouted, "It's time!"

The ship's ramp dropped with a great splash.

"Let's move!" another voice boomed. "Go!"

Walt and the other men hurried down the ramp. One after another, they plunged into the frigid sea.

The water was up to Walt's chest. Other men leaped into the waves and disappeared. Had their heavy packs pulled them under?

Walt hesitated. A deep voice from behind him boomed, "You're not a rescue ship! Get onshore!"

"Keep your gun dry!" someone else shouted.

Walt held his rifle high over his head and stumbled forward. All around him, men staggered and fell. He didn't know if they'd been shot or knocked over by waves. There was no time to find out.

He had to keep going.

He had to make it to the beach.

## Chapter 2

# EARLY MORNING THUNDER

In a village just over the ridge from the sea, Leo Rubinstein sat up in bed. Thundering booms rattled the windows. Was there a storm? His sister Rebecca's black-and-white cat, Belle, jumped from his mattress to the floor.

"Henri!" a deep voice called from the kitchen.

Leo stood up. He was finally getting used to being called Henri. When Mémère, his grandmother, had dropped him off at this farm two years ago, he'd understood that it was no longer safe to be Leo Rubinstein, the Jewish boy from Paris. Now he was Henri Blanc, a Catholic boy staying with his uncle in Normandy for a while to help out on the farm.

Leo felt the lie poke at him every time he had to tell it. But the truth was too dangerous. Nazi soldiers and the French police who worked with them were rounding up Jewish people all over France, taking them . . . well, no one was certain where. When Leo asked, Mémère only told him to pray that the Allies would come soon to defeat the Nazis so they could all be free again.

So Leo had prayed. He'd wished and hoped and prayed some more. He'd listened to the BBC radio reports when it was safe. He'd even tried to learn English from one of his father's university books, so he could talk to the American and English soldiers if they really came.

Another blast shook the sky. Was this the day?

Leo dressed and rushed downstairs. Mr. and Mrs. Blanc were in the kitchen, loading a basket with dried meats and bread.

"What's happening?" Leo asked.

"It has begun." Mr. Blanc tucked a satchel of coins into his sack. "The Allies are here to liberate France."

"They really came!" Leo's heart leaped.

But Mrs. Blanc said, "Now is no time to celebrate, with bombs falling from the sky. We must go!" She picked up the basket, made a sign of the cross, and pushed Leo toward the door.

"Go where?" If they weren't safe in the sturdy farmhouse, Leo couldn't imagine where they would be.

"The radio said find a ditch or make one,"

Mrs. Blanc said as they hurried through the morning rain, past the garden. "I sent the older boys out to start." She pointed. Leo spotted Pierre and Michel digging with shovels way out in the field.

"You go on," Mr. Blanc told his wife. "Henri, come with me to free the animals."

"What?" Leo was shocked. Last year, German soldiers had taken away the Blancs' horses to transport supplies. The family depended on their cows and chickens. Since the war started, there was never enough food to buy at the market. They were even forced to give away their milk. The Germans demanded five liters a day. Pierre and Michel always stuck their fingers in the milk to put germs in it before they delivered it to the soldiers. "How will we get milk if we let the cows go?" Leo asked.

"Better to set them free than see them crushed under debris when the next bomb falls," Mr. Blanc said as they ran to the barn.

The animals already knew something was wrong. The chickens were squawking and fretting. The cows stomped nervously at the dirt. When Leo opened the gate, they practically stampeded into the road.

When the last animal was freed, Mr. Blanc told Leo, "Go to the ditch now. I need to help old Mr. Dufort with his horses. I will be there soon."

Leo nodded. He started running through the mud toward the ditch. But he paused to look up at the house. Could it really be bombed as the Allies advanced? How could the people they'd been waiting and hoping for end up doing them harm?

Then Leo caught a flash of black and white in the window. Belle!

He darted back into the house and scooped up the cat. "You must come with us. Rebecca would never forgive me if I let harm come to you." Leo swallowed hard. He didn't know when he'd see his parents or sister again, but taking care of his sister's cat felt like a promise that it might happen someday.

Leo ran to the window and searched the sky for planes. There was smoke, but nothing else he could see. So instead of going straight to the ditch, he ran down to the basement and pulled a flour canister from the shelf.

Leo set Belle down carefully beside him and unscrewed the lid. The can wasn't really full of flour; it held the crystal radio that Mr. Blanc used to listen to the BBC radio broadcasts from England. That was forbidden by the Nazis, so every time the Blancs wanted news, they sent Leo out to the garden to play. Really, he was watching for German soldiers. He'd run inside to warn Mr. Blanc if any were coming.

Leo fiddled with the radio, hoping for news.

Was it really happening now? How long would it take the Allies to defeat the Nazis? Where was his family, and when would they be together again? Leo turned the buttons, but there was only static.

Belle let out a meow, and then Leo heard another sound. A low buzz. It wasn't coming from the radio.

Leo dropped the radio, grabbed the cat, and raced up the stairs to a window.

Two warplanes roared through the sky.

They were headed straight for the house.

## Chapter 3

## RACE TO THE WAVES

"Race you to the water!" Luke called across the beach to Sadie, who was working on a sand castle.

"No fair! You got a head start!" Sadie shouted. She jumped to her feet and ran after him, splashing into the lake. "Come swim with us, Ranger!"

Ranger looked up from the hole he was digging in the sand. Lakeshore holes were the very best kind to dig. The wet sand was soft, and no one yelled at him about messing up the garden. But the water looked like fun, too.

Ranger backed out of his hole and started toward the waves. But then a white-and-gray bird caught his eye.

*Seagull!*

Ranger barked and ran toward it. The seagull started running, too.

Ranger ran faster. He'd almost caught up when the bird unfolded its wings and flew away over the sand. Ranger barked once more. Then he headed for the water to join Luke and Sadie.

"Nice try, Ranger!" Luke said as Ranger splashed up to him. "But birds are even harder to catch than squirrels. Flying and all." He gave Ranger a damp pat on the head.

Ranger knew about birds and flying. He loved chasing seagulls anyway, just like he loved chasing squirrels at home. That was the reason he was playing at the beach today and not off on an official search-and-rescue mission somewhere.

Ranger had done all kinds of search-and-rescue dog training with Luke and his dad. He'd learned to track missing people by following the scent trails they left behind. He'd learned how to search for people who were hurt in fallen-down buildings and how to bring back help. But in order to be an official search-and-rescue dog, you had to pass a special test. You had to follow a scent and ignore everything else in your path. Even hot dogs! Even squirrels!

Ranger had managed to trot past the hot dog on his test day, but when a twitchy-tailed squirrel ran across the field, he'd taken off chasing it. Ranger knew there wasn't a real person in trouble that day. It was just practice again. If a real person had needed help, Ranger would have left the squirrel alone and helped.

But that didn't matter. Ranger didn't pass his test, so here he was at the beach, and that was fine. Ranger loved the beach. He splashed around with Sadie and Luke and curled up in the sun until it was time to go home.

When the car pulled into the driveway, Ranger followed everyone into the house. He stopped in the mudroom to get a drink from his water dish, but it was empty. Ranger barked, and Luke came and took his dish away to fill it. But before Luke came back, Ranger heard a familiar sound coming from his dog bed.

Ranger nuzzled his blanket aside until he found the old first aid kit he'd dug up from the garden one day. It was humming quietly — something that happened every once in a while, when someone far away was in trouble. The last time the old metal box hummed, it had taken Ranger to a trembling place where a girl named Lily needed help. The time before that, Ranger had found himself in the middle of a rainstorm with a girl named Helga in a land of smoke and ash. Before that, the old box had brought him to a ship bound for the South Pole, where a boy named Jack was starting a dangerous journey.

Ranger looked up. On the wall over his dog bed was a drawing Jack had made of him. Ranger pawed at his blanket some more and uncovered a bright yellow feather — a gift of thanks from Lily after he'd helped her escape from a great earthquake and fire.

Now the first aid kit was humming again.

Ranger nuzzled its old leather strap over his neck. He whined as the humming buzzed louder. The box grew warm at his neck, and light shone out from the cracks. It got brighter and brighter until Ranger couldn't see his dog bed or the mudroom anymore. *Too bright!* He had to close his eyes, and the skin on his neck prickled. He felt as if he was being squeezed through a hole in the sky.

Finally, the humming stopped. There was a quick half second of quiet before the air exploded with booms, blasts, and splashes. Deep voices cried out.

Ranger opened his eyes. Sand sprayed into them. Something whistled past his ear with a sharp zing.

Ranger's paws sank into the wet sand. He was on a beach, but there was no time to guess where or why. He wasn't home and he wasn't safe. No one was.

Men ran everywhere. Shouting. Stumbling. Falling to the sand. Those who stayed on their feet were all running away from the waves, toward a shallow, rocky ditch.

Ranger raced after them.

# Chapter 4

## CHAOS AND SAND

Ranger leaped into the ditch. He skidded down loose rocks and nearly landed on one of the men — a tall, skinny soldier with dark brown skin. The young man's green-brown clothes and pack dripped with seawater as he crouched, trying to catch his breath.

"We brought dogs in the first wave of boats?" he called to another man.

The other man shrugged and wiped blood from his cheek. "Guess so. Probably for the land mines. Captain said the whole beach up there is loaded. You got dry ammo, Walt?"

The man called Walt nodded and handed the other man a small box. While the other man loaded his gun, Walt reached for the first aid kit around Ranger's neck. Ranger watched as he opened the box and shook his head at the little collection of bandages and gauze inside. "Afraid we'll need a lot more than this today," Walt said. He closed the box and tucked it away beside some other supplies.

Ranger shook the rain from his fur and looked around. Everywhere, soldiers were running, falling, stumbling into the ditch out of breath while the air seemed to explode around them. Where was he? And how was he supposed to help these wet, frightened men?

Ranger walked along the ditch, slipping through the chaotic crowd. Men shouted over the noise to one another. Some rummaged through their packs, reloading guns.

One was curled up against the rocks, knees to his chest, with his eyes squeezed shut.

More and more men spilled into the ditch until there was no more room at all. Gunfire rattled over their heads. Something exploded nearby and sent another blast of sand spraying into Ranger's eyes.

"We have to get off this beach!" one of the men shouted. "Come on!"

"Ready?" someone else yelled. "Go!"

The men at the far end of the ditch scrambled out onto the sand and started running. Ranger climbed up a bit to see where they were headed. Something whistled past his ear and he fell back. He couldn't tell where the men were going, but in that split second above the sand, he'd seen enough to know they weren't safe.

Dark smoke filled the air. Soldiers raced up the beach, dodging jagged pieces of metal that jutted up from the sand. They jumped over nests of sharp, snarled wires. Everywhere, men were falling.

And the noise! Booms and blasts shook the sky. It was even louder than the fireworks at home that made Ranger duck under Luke's bed. Here, there was no place to hide.

How was Ranger supposed to help? His other journeys hadn't prepared him for the chaos of this terrifying beach. In all the times his first aid kit had hummed, all the times it had taken him far away to help someone in trouble, he'd never seen anything like this.

"Look out! Make room!"

Two more men came tumbling into the ditch, dripping wet, hugging their guns to their chests.

"Where's Jackson?" one of them said. "He was right behind me on the ramp."

The other man shook his head. "They let us

out too deep! We must have lost half a dozen men soon as they hit the water."

"We have to go back!" someone shouted.

Ranger looked up. It was Walt, the tall, skinny man he'd seen earlier.

"Come on!" Walt crept to the edge of the ditch and looked over the rim. Something exploded, and pieces of metal came showering into the ditch.

"Get down, Walt! We can't go back! We'll never make it!" one of the other men shouted.

Ranger pawed at the Walt man's pant leg to get him to come back down where it was safer. But Walt hoisted himself up. He left his gun in the ditch and ran back toward the churning ocean.

Ranger felt an unmistakable tug to follow, even though the air still boomed with gunfire. He jumped out of the ditch, paws slipping on the wet sand, and ran after Walt.

## Chapter 5

# RESCUE FROM THE SEA

Walt couldn't run very fast with the weight of his wet pack, so Ranger caught up quickly. Walt didn't look down. His eyes were trained on the water. He didn't stop when he reached the waves. He splashed in, sinking into the wet sand in his boots. Soon he was up to his waist, plunging his arms into the waves.

Ranger bounded into the sea, too. A wave swept his paws out from under him. He paddled against the current, struggling to keep his nose out of the water.

The air was thick with smells — salt water

and smoke. Chemicals and blood and fear. Ranger caught Walt's scent mixed with the smells of other men. Ranger could tell some of those men were still in the water.

Again, Walt reached deep into the crashing waves. This time, he tugged and staggered back. He pulled again and lugged a soldier from the water by the arm. The man was shorter than Walt but much heavier. Ranger wanted to help, but all he could do was watch as Walt dragged the man to the beach.

Walt knelt and pounded the man's chest. He blew two long breaths into the man's mouth. Walt did that again and again until the man coughed up water and rolled onto his side.

"Come on!" Walt tugged at the man's arms, pulling him to his feet. "Get to cover!" Walt held the man up as they staggered back to the rocky ditch and collapsed.

One of the other soldiers clapped Walt on the shoulder. "You saved him!"

Ranger waited for Walt to go back, to help the other men. But Walt reached for his pack.

Ranger barked. There were more men still out in the water. Two of them. Ranger had smelled their sweat and their breath and their fear. But he couldn't save them without Walt's help.

Ranger barked again. Walt ignored him, or maybe he couldn't hear over the rattling gunfire that still pounded the beach.

Ranger pawed at Walt. He jumped up on him and pushed him with his front legs.

Walt swatted him away. "Get out of here, dog!"

But Ranger barked again. He jumped out of the ditch and ran toward the water. Then he ran back to Walt, barking. He ran back and forth until finally, Walt turned and stared into the waves.

"Are there more?" Walt said. Ranger knew Walt wasn't talking to him, but he understood one word.

*More!* That was a command from Ranger's search-and-rescue training. Sometimes, when he was practicing to find people trapped in fallen-down buildings, he'd find Luke hiding in a big pipe or under a wooden box. Usually, that meant Ranger's work was done, and it was time to go home. But sometimes, Luke or Dad would point him back to the rubble and say, "Find more!" That meant more people needed help. Just like they did today.

*More! Find more!*

Ranger barked again. He raced back into the waves, hoping Walt would follow. He tracked the men's scents to the spot where he'd been before. The salt water splashed into his eyes and stung them, but Ranger dived into the waves again and again. Finally, his paws touched something solid. Ranger lifted his head out of the waves. He barked and barked until Walt came running back into the sea.

Walt dragged two more men onto the beach. He pounded their chests until they coughed up water and breathed again. Then another man came and helped Walt drag them both through the gunfire to a safer spot.

Ranger stayed by Walt's side. When they finally made it out of the gunfire and into the ditch, Walt leaned back and looked up at the sky, breathing hard. He put a hand on Ranger's neck and ruffled his wet fur. "You had my back out there, didn't you, dog?"

Ranger leaned into Walt and waited for something to happen. He could see his first aid kit, half buried in the sand of the ditch along with someone's pack. He'd found a way

to help, but the old metal box was still quiet. There was no humming sound, letting him know his job was done. That meant there was more work to do before he could go home.

The gunfire quieted for a moment, but then a new sound filled the sky. A buzz and then a growl of airplanes. Two of them roared overhead. The planes passed over a ridge and disappeared. There was a whistle, then an enormous blast. Even far away, it shook the sand under Ranger's paws.

Smoke and dust rose into the sky. What had happened? Ranger's skin prickled, and he knew his work wasn't done.

He scrambled out of the ditch and raced over the beach toward the ridge.

## Chapter 6

## A PROMISE KEPT

Ranger ran up the beach, dodging sharp bits of metal that jutted out of the sand. The air was full of smoke and noise. At the bottom of a steep hill, Ranger came to a tiny box of a house, made of concrete. The skin on his neck prickled. The windows of the building had guns instead of glass. The men inside wore clothes that were different from Walt's. Different from the other men on the beach.

Ranger crouched low and slipped past them, behind the building, and up the hill. His paws slipped in the mud, but he climbed to the top. A village spread out in the gray morning light. Its streets were lined with small shops and houses and a little stone church. At the edge of the village, thick smoke rose from a heaping pile of rocks and timbers.

Ranger raced down the hill through the weeds and brush. Pricker bushes grabbed at his fur, but Ranger pushed through until he came to a big field with another ditch full of people. They were quieter and dressed differently than any of the men on the beach. Here, there were women and children. Ranger leaped over the ditch at a narrow spot and headed for the billowing smoke.

When he got to the rubble pile, he stopped. Was it a house? Whatever it was, something had crushed it. Were the people who lived here safe out in the ditch? Or was someone trapped underneath the heaps of stone and wood?

Ranger stepped carefully onto a plank at

the edge of the mess. It wobbled, and he had to shift his weight to balance. Somewhere in the mess of crushed furniture and splintered wood, there was a creak and then a thump. This site wasn't stable. Ranger knew from his training that fallen-down buildings were dangerous places to search.

Ranger had practiced this kind of searching with Luke and his dad. He'd practiced moving safely over all kinds of surfaces. He'd balanced on planks and walked over old car hoods and bedsprings. He'd crawled through dark tunnels and climbed up ladders. Sometimes, he and Luke went to the playground so Ranger could walk over the seesaw. He'd climb up and down the metal slide and practice spreading his toes so he wouldn't slip back down.

But this was no playground. Ranger leaped onto a pile of rocks. He smelled smoke and sharp chemicals, but also a trace of food from the night before — meat and apples and bread. Ranger circled the outside of the pile of rubble. That way he would be sure to catch the scent of any people trapped in the timbers and stones.

He climbed over a pile of boards and down into a low, open space that must have been a kitchen once. A toppled cabinet had sent dishes shattering over the wooden floor. Ranger stepped carefully between the chunks of pottery and jagged shards of glass. The smells were stronger here. That happened sometimes in low places where scents pooled, out of the wind. Ranger could smell the same smoke and food but also . . . cat?

He climbed over the cabinet and sniffed again. Definitely cat.

Ranger made his way around the edge of the kitchen space. He jumped over what was left of a chimney.

"Mreeeow!" A black-and-white cat perched on a rough chunk of rock, staring at him. It looked like Ruggles, the cat that lived next door to Luke and Sadie. But this cat's fur was wet and matted. One of its ears was smaller than the other. It wore a tiny bell on a muddy blue ribbon around its neck.

Ranger barked at the cat. It didn't move. Then the wind shifted, and he caught a new scent in the air. A person smell!

Ranger padded carefully around the fallen chimney and sniffed again. The person scent was stronger here. He climbed over another tumbled beam and found a boy curled up in a corner. The boy looked about Luke's age, but his hair was darker, and he was a lot skinnier. The boy wasn't trapped under anything, but his eyes were closed.

It wasn't safe to stay here. Not with bits of

the house still settling and falling. Ranger barked, but the boy didn't wake up.

Ranger barked again and licked him on the cheek. The boy's face twitched. Ranger pawed at his shoulder until the boy opened his eyes. "Where'd you come from, dog?" he whispered. And then, "Where's Belle?"

Ranger didn't know what the boy was saying, but he knew they had to get away from these teetering stones and unsteady beams. He pawed the boy's shoulder until he stood up.

"Belle? Belle!" the boy called.

There was a jingle from behind them. The boy whipped around and dropped to his knees.

"You're here!" All at once, the boy was laughing and crying and hugging the not-Ruggles cat. "Thank goodness I didn't lose you for good. I kept my promise." He wiped at the tears on his cheeks.

Ranger barked, and the boy looked up. "Are you lost, too, dog? I'm Leo." He patted Ranger on the head with his cat-smelling hand and whispered, "It's good that you can't give away secrets. I'm supposed to tell people here my name is Henri. Who do you belong to? I wonder —"

The Leo boy stopped talking and stared past Ranger into the sky.

Ranger heard a sound that prickled the fur on his neck. It was the quiet buzz from before, getting louder again, and louder. Ranger looked up. There was no ceiling left in Leo's house, so nothing blocked the chilling view of the sky.

Five more planes soared in formation over the smoking countryside. They were getting closer by the second.

# Chapter 7

## SMOKE AND BOMBS

"Bombers!" Leo shouted. He scooped up the cat, jumped to his feet, and stumbled over the stones. "Come on, dog! Run to the ditch!"

Ranger leaped out of the rubble and waited at the edge of the house. The planes made a loud rumble that rattled him from his paws to his tail. They were coming closer by the second. The boy needed to hurry. Ranger barked at him.

Leo scrambled over a jumble of fallen shelves. He had to put Belle down to climb through a heap of stones that used to be the pantry. The planes droned louder and louder. Belle leaped over a fallen beam and tore through the garden.

"Belle, no!" Leo hoisted himself up and chased after her, tripping through the broken rocks.

The planes roared, almost overhead. Ranger barked. Faster! Or they'd never make it to the ditch in time!

Leo pumped his legs as hard as he could, sloshing through the wet field with the shaggy golden dog beside him. He couldn't see Belle anymore. He could only hope she'd run to the ditch where Mr. and Mrs. Blanc were waiting.

Leo sucked in great gulps of damp morning air. His legs burned. The planes were screaming overhead. Why couldn't he run faster?

Then Leo's foot caught on a rock and he flew forward. *Whumph!* He landed on his stomach in the mud and couldn't breathe at all.

The planes were deafening. Leo didn't dare look. He curled into a ball, as small as he could, and covered his head with his arms. Ranger crouched low beside him.

The bombers roared so low they shook the earth.

But nothing fell. There was no blast this time. The planes thundered over them and continued inland.

Leo finally caught his breath and tipped his head up to look. The planes were already growing smaller. Where were they headed? He thought of his grandparents and his mother, still in Paris as far as he knew, and said a quiet prayer for their safety. For all of his family's safety, wherever they were. And then he thought of his older sister, Rebecca. Where was her cat?

Leo stood and started trudging through the field again. "Belle! Where'd you go, Belle?"

Ranger walked alongside him, and after a few minutes, they came to a shallow ditch. It looked like someone had dug it quickly. Shovels were tossed on the ground nearby. But whoever had been here was gone now.

It wasn't as deep as the other ditch, on the beach, but it was better than nothing. They needed shelter, even though the planes were gone for now. Ranger nudged Leo toward the ditch.

Leo pushed back. He squinted into the distance and thought he saw a flash of white in the thick bushes along the ridge near the beach. Leo hesitated. It was smokier and louder over that way. The Allies and Germans must be fighting near the sea. And what if the bombers returned? It would be safer to take cover, but Leo had to keep the promise he'd made to Rebecca the last time he'd seen her.

That was two summers ago, on the day of the roundup. Leo remembered as if it were yesterday. How could he forget the banging at their apartment door? French police dragged his entire family out of bed that morning, marched them away, and crammed them into a crowded truck that brought them to the Vélodrome d'Hiver, the big cycling stadium near the Eiffel Tower. The police packed the stadium with thousands of Jewish men, women, and children. There was no food or water for two days. Leo's eyes and throat burned with the awful smells of too many people with nowhere to use the bathroom.

Leo's mother had been sick before they left.

Her cough grew deeper and more rattly by the hour. Finally, his father convinced an officer to send her to see a doctor at the hospital. Leo was sent along to care for her.

As he left, Rebecca said, "If you get back to the apartment, you must feed Belle."

"All right," Leo said, and started to go.

But Rebecca clutched his wrist. Her eyes shone with tears. "Be safe," she whispered. "Care for her. And for yourself."

"I will. I promise." Then Leo followed the soldiers who loaded his mother into a truck and drove her to the hospital across town. They put her in a crowded room with five other women.

The following morning, Leo's mémère arrived. Somehow, she'd learned they were at the hospital. She kissed Leo on the cheeks, then sat by his mother's bed and stroked her hair. When the doctor stepped out, there were whispered words between Mémère and his mother.

The next thing Leo knew, Mémère was hurrying him out of the hospital and through the crowded streets. He spent the night at his grandparents' small apartment. In the morning, they hurried down the block to the empty apartment Leo's family had left the day before. Mémère packed up some clothes for Leo. She carefully removed the yellow star from his jacket.

"But, Mémère," Leo said, "won't I get in trouble with the police?" The Nazis required Jews to wear a yellow star and carry identity papers at all times.

"Hush," Mémère whispered. "Come with me."

Leo scooped up Belle under one arm and tucked her into the bag with his clothing. Thankfully, the old cat was quiet. Mémère rushed Leo through the city streets to the train station, gripping his hand as they walked past German soldiers at the gate. They boarded a train bound for Normandy. Mémère's eyes darted everywhere. Leo didn't dare to speak.

It was only when the train chugged away and the buildings of Paris gave way to fields and farmhouses that Mémère seemed to breathe again. It wasn't safe in Paris anymore, she explained as they rattled through the countryside. And it wasn't safe to be Jewish *anywhere*. Leo would have to pretend to be a Catholic boy helping on his uncle's farm. Leo was good at pretending, Mémère reminded him. It wouldn't be forever.

Whenever it felt safe enough, Mémère had come to see him on the farm. She'd visited several times in the two years since she'd left him. Every time, Leo asked when he could go home.

Mémère's answer was always the same. Soon, she hoped. Soon.

When Leo asked about his mother, his father, and his sister, Mémère only said they should pray. Pray for the Allies to come soon, and hopefully one day, they might be together again.

Today, in a morning of smoke and bombs, the Allies had finally arrived. Leo held his hand over his eyes to block the sun and stared off into the distance.

He caught a glimpse of Belle's black-and-white tail swishing in the leaves and took off running toward the beach.

## Chapter 8

# DANGER IN THE SHADOWS

Ranger raced in front of Leo and tried to block his way. The smoky beach wasn't safe! But Leo pushed Ranger aside and kept running.

When they reached the row of pricker bushes where Leo thought he'd seen the cat, he crouched low and whistled. "Belle?" he called, pushing branches aside. But the cat wasn't there. Leo climbed higher on the ridge to see where she might have gone. He hoisted himself over a rocky ledge, stood up, and gasped.

Leo dropped to the ground and stared out toward the water. His heart thudded against his ribs as he tried to take in the scene spread out before him.

Everywhere he looked, soldiers with rifles pressed to their shoulders were aiming up into the cliffs. Huge trucks crawled over the beach. Skeletons of burned-out tanks littered the shore. The sea was clogged with ships of every size. Wave after wave of soldiers spilled from the boats and surged onto the sand. Leo's beautiful beach, with its cool winds and crashing waves, had exploded into a mess of smoke and twisted metal.

Leo's heart sank. Belle always lurked under the bed when the farmhouse was too noisy. He would never find her in the middle of this chaos. She was probably scared to death. Unless she'd found someplace to hide . . .

Leo crept forward on his hands and knees to a higher spot on the ridge. His hands were scraped, and the bushes scratched at his belly

through his shirt. But maybe from here, he could see where she might have gone.

Just down the hill was a pillbox, a little concrete building where soldiers took shelter. The Germans had built them all up and down the coast because they knew the Allied forces might come across the English Channel by boat.

This one sat quietly now. Was it empty? It would be cool and dark inside — just the kind of place Belle loved to hide. But what if someone else was hiding there?

Leo picked up a rock the size of a small apple. He took a deep breath and threw it into a thicket near the pillbox. Then he ducked low and waited.

If there were German soldiers inside, they'd come out to investigate, wouldn't they? They'd have to make sure that noise wasn't an enemy hiding in the brush. Leo waited with his heart pounding.

The pillbox sat quiet and undisturbed.

Carefully, slowly, Leo crept down the hill on his knees and elbows, belly to the ground.

Ranger followed him. He was good at staying down. He'd practiced climbing under obstacles in his training with Luke and Dad. Soon, they were down the hill, beside the bushes at the edge of the little building.

Leo crawled toward the entrance to the pillbox. "Belle?" he whispered. "Are you in there, girl?"

Ranger sniffed the air. He caught the scent of several men who had come this way. But those scent trails weren't fresh.

"Belle? Come on out!" Leo whispered as he approached the door.

Ranger crept closer to the concrete box and lifted his nose again. Smoke choked the air and made it harder for him to pick out other smells, but . . . *There!*

A man smell drifted out from the box.

Ranger barked. But it was too late.

"Don't move!" a rough voice shouted.

Leo froze. A soldier appeared in the doorway, aiming a rifle down at him.

## Chapter 9

## ENEMY OR FRIEND?

Leo stared up at the soldier, a tall, skinny man with short black hair and brown skin. His uniform didn't look like the ones worn by the German soldiers who patrolled Leo's village. Could he be one of the Allies?

"S'il vous plaît, Monsieur! Je cherche mon chat!" Leo blurted. He lifted his hands so the soldier could see he meant no harm, and spoke the words in English, too. "Please, sir . . . I am looking for my cat."

The man's face softened, but he didn't lower

his gun. He motioned for Leo to come into the boxy shelter. Ranger went, too.

"Is this dog yours?" the man asked in English.

Leo was so relieved to know this wasn't a German soldier that he almost forgot to answer. When the soldier pointed to the dog, Leo said, "No. I thought he was one of the war dogs." Leo had heard about dogs that helped soldiers in battle.

The soldier lowered his gun and held out his hand.

Ranger sniffed it. This was the Walt man from the ditch on the beach. He'd lost his helmet and gotten a lot dirtier, but Ranger recognized his scent. He licked the man's hand, and the soldier gave him a rough pat on the head.

"Must be," Walt said. "Dog was on the

beach first thing this morning. Lord knows what became of his handler." The soldier looked out of the pillbox and over the sand. The gunfire had quieted, but fallen men were everywhere. Walt wondered if whoever brought the dog ashore was among them.

Leo leaned against the shelter's cool concrete wall. Ranger sat down beside him.

"You speak good English," the soldier said.

Leo shrugged. "A bit. I practiced so I could talk to the Allies when they came." He looked up at the man. "Are you American?"

Walt nodded. "Sergeant Walter Burrell of the 320th. Where do you live?" he asked.

Leo pointed over the ridge toward what was left of the Blancs' farmhouse.

"What's your name?" the soldier asked.

Leo's voice caught in his throat. Earlier today, he would have said it was Henri Blanc, just as he'd told people for the past two years.

But the Allies had come. Could he tell the truth now? "My name is Leo Rubinstein," Leo whispered. "No one here knows that," he added. "I lived in Paris. It was bad there. When Mémère brought me here, she told me to call myself Henri, to be safe."

"No name's going to keep you safe wandering around a battlefield. You're lucky you didn't come over that ridge fifteen minutes ago when we were flushing Nazis out of this pillbox. We need to get you home. And I have to get back to my balloon."

"Balloon?" Leo was confused.

Walt pointed out the window opening. In the distance, Leo saw two men holding on to ropes, trying to control a big, silvery thing in the sky. It looked like a giant gray potato with a tail — nothing like any balloon Leo had seen. "What is it?" he asked.

"A barrage balloon." Walt spoke as he

gathered up supplies that the Germans had left behind in the shelter. He tucked boxes of bullets and matches into his pack on the ground. "We're raising a curtain of them over the beach for protection."

"What?" Leo asked. The soldier was speaking so quickly that it was hard for Leo to understand much.

"We stagger the balloons," Walt said. "It forces German planes to fly higher, so their aim isn't so good for bombing. When they're flying higher, they're better targets for our big guns on the ground, too."

Leo stared out at the men wrestling with the balloon on the windy beach. It tugged and pulled at its ropes. Leo was searching his mind for the right English words to ask more about it when he heard a jingle in the bushes.

"Belle!" Leo ran from the pillbox, dived into a bush, and pulled out the black-and-white cat. She let out an angry "Mrreow!" but settled down when Leo stroked the fur between her ears. He carried her back into the little shelter and announced, "I found my cat. I will go home now. Or . . ." Leo swallowed hard. Home was far away in Paris. Even his temporary home with the Blancs was gone now. "I will go back to the field. We dug a ditch . . ."

Walt shook his head. "The fighting has moved over the ridge, but we may not have liberated your village yet. It's not safe. I'll come back when I've finished my work and take you then. Stay here for now." He hoisted his pack onto his shoulders. "And stay down. Just because the Germans are gone doesn't mean they won't be back."

"Where are you going?" Leo asked.

"Back to the beach," Walt answered. He slapped his thigh with his hand. "Come on, dog. I need your help."

## Chapter 10

# THROUGH THE MINEFIELD

Walt stepped outside the pillbox. He took a deep, shaky breath and looked toward the beach.

Just a few hours ago, he'd been one of a dozen men who marched up this sandy shelf that led to the plateau. But this stretch of beach was full of buried land mines, hidden dangers that exploded with one wrong step. Only four of the twelve men had made it through. They'd fought their way up to the pillbox and taken the two German soldiers who had been there as prisoners. The other three American soldiers had taken those men to a holding area.

Now, to get back to his balloon crew, Walt had to cross that deadly stretch of sand again. He started walking away from the pillbox at a good pace but quickly slowed to a stop. He looked at the uneven sand in front of him. Then he looked at Ranger.

Walt had never worked with the military dogs trained to sniff for the explosives in land mines. He'd heard that they would stop when they came to a mine. That was how it was supposed to work anyway. He could only pray this dog was trained well.

Walt gave Ranger a pat on his neck. "Go ahead, dog."

Ranger looked up. He could tell the soldier wanted him to do something, but he wasn't sure what. "Go ahead, dog" wasn't a command he'd learned from Luke or Dad in training.

The soldier didn't seem to be looking for anyone. He just seemed worried about the sand. What was Ranger supposed to do about that?

"Go on, then." Walt patted Ranger's backside and pointed over the stretch of beach.

Ranger sniffed the air. It was still smoky, but at least most of the booming had stopped. He took a careful step forward. The sand was wet from the morning rains. It felt squishy and gritty under his paws.

Ranger took another step and sniffed at the sand. It smelled wet and earthy and fishy, just like the beach at home. But here, there were other scents, too. Boots and gasoline, sickness and sweat and blood.

Ranger stepped forward again. Walt stayed close behind him.

He kept his nose low, creeping over the beach.

*There!*

Ranger stopped and sniffed.

Something was off.

Different.

Just ahead, the sand had a strange chemical scent. Ranger had smelled it once before. After one of his search-and-rescue training sessions with Luke and Dad, some men had visited to see which dogs might be good at a different kind of work. They'd waved a package under Ranger's nose. It had smelled a lot like this sand — earthy and dangerous and sharp.

The men taught Ranger and a few other dogs to find that particular scent. The dogs sniffed packages, and if they sat down when they smelled it, they got a treat. The next time the men came to visit, they brought a fancy spinning wheel with slots for four containers. Two of the slots were empty. One had food hidden inside — it smelled like hot dogs to

Ranger — and one had a package with the funny, sharp smell. Ranger was good at finding the scent. Almost every time the men spun the wheel, Ranger pawed at the right slot, sat down, and earned his treat.

Here in the sand, the smell was mixed with other things, but it was the same scent. Ranger could tell. He sat down, looked up at Walt, and waited for his reward.

Walt didn't pull a dog treat out of his pocket. Instead, he squinted at the sand. After a few seconds, he let out a long, shaky breath, put a trembling hand on Ranger's head, and said, "Good dog. Good job."

He turned Ranger away from the strange-smelling sand and waited for Ranger to go ahead again. Ranger crept forward, sniffing at the beach. He understood what his job was now. He tried not to pay attention to all of the other smells. He and Walt passed close to two

men sprawled in the sand, all crumpled and still. But he kept going.

Twice more, Ranger found the earthy chemical smell in the sand just ahead of them. Both times, he stopped and sat down, and Walt circled them around the spot.

"This should be about the end of it," Walt said. Ranger stayed in front, but they moved along more quickly. The sand grew rockier, with smooth pebbles mixed in. The rush of the sea grew louder. Ranger paused and lifted his head. The ocean was so much closer now! It had swallowed up most of the beach that had been there this morning.

"Walt! Hurry!" someone shouted over the roar of the sea. Two men were staggering through the waves, walking one of the giant, silvery balloons to shore from a boat. The balloon tugged at its cables as if it were a wild, flying dog on a leash.

"Hold on!" Walt started forward, but Ranger darted in front of him. He was supposed to go first. That was how it worked.

Ranger sniffed at the sand.

*There!*

Ranger sat down, but Walt's eyes were fixed on the balloon men. He didn't stop and circle carefully around. He nudged at Ranger. "Go on, dog! They need my help."

Ranger barked again, but it didn't matter.

Walt pushed forward through the sand.

## Chapter 11

# UP AND AWAY!

Ranger barked again. He'd given the signal. Why wasn't Walt listening?

*No!*

*Stop!*

*There!*

Ranger jumped up on Walt and pushed him backward with his paws. Walt stumbled but didn't fall.

Ranger sat and kept barking.

Walt froze. His eyes darted back and forth from Ranger to the balloon men. Then he

75

stared hard at the patch of sand just ahead and sucked in his breath. "Good job, dog."

Slowly, Walt and Ranger circled around the funny-smelling spot. Walt stayed back and waited for Ranger to sniff their way through the rest of the sand.

The strange smells faded away. Ranger stayed alert, but he moved more quickly, and soon they reached the ridge of smooth stones where they'd taken shelter before. The two men with the balloon still struggled to control it. Whipping winds threatened to rip the cables from their hands.

"We need to bring it down for now!" one of the men shouted.

"Hold on!" Walt called. "I'll grab the other mooring line!" He threw off his pack and pulled out two pairs of gloves — one made of rubber and one made of leather. Pulling them on took precious time, but both were crucial.

Without the leather gloves, the cables would rip his hands. The rubber gloves underneath saved him from getting shocked by static electricity when he handled the steel lines.

Another gust caught the balloon. The men struggled to hold on. One of the soldiers lost his footing in the wet sand and fell forward. He clung to the cable, and the balloon dragged him over the beach. The other mooring lines whipped in the wind.

Ranger raced to one of the loose cables. He tried to catch it, but the wind twisted it away. The gritty, sandy metal slapped against Ranger's snout, but he leaped into the air again. This time, Ranger caught the end of the cable in his mouth. He turned and raced toward Walt. The steel cable scratched at Ranger's mouth, but he held on until Walt caught the line firmly in his gloved hands.

"Got it!" Walt pulled the cable as tight as he could.

The other soldier had never let go, even as the cable had jerked him over the sand. He scrambled to his feet and shouted, "Let's bring it in!"

"Careful now!" Walt called. Together, the men pulled in the cables. Finally, the wind seemed to give up on the balloon, and they brought it down onto the top of a truck. They covered it with a net and secured the lines to sandbags on both sides to keep the balloon weighted down.

Ranger sat on the beach and watched the men do a final check of the lines. His mouth was all scratched and sandy from the cable. He was thirsty, too, but the only water here was the salty ocean. Ranger felt a wave splash his tail and turned around. The sea had crept up behind him while the men worked. Waves lapped at the pack Walt had dropped on the beach.

Ranger barked, but Walt was busy lugging sandbags. Ranger trotted over to the pack, took the strap in his teeth, and tugged it out of the waves. He dragged it all the way to Walt's feet and barked again.

"You got that mutt trained pretty well, don't you?" one of the other men said.

"He's not mine," Walt answered. He bent and scratched Ranger behind his ear. "No clue where he came from, but he's been looking out for me all right."

Ranger leaned into the scratch. He liked Walt, but he missed Luke's scratches. Ranger was hungry and thirsty, and his nose still stung from where the cable had slapped at him. When would he get to go home?

"Come on, dog. Let's get to some shelter,"

Walt said. He hoisted his pack over his shoulder and started following the other men back to the protected area behind the ridge of stones. Ranger trotted close beside him. It wasn't as loud as it had been earlier. The rattle of gunfire was more distant. Every so often, a shell explosion would echo over the sand. But the constant booms had mostly been replaced with work sounds — the rumble of trucks and the shouts of officers giving orders to men moving supplies.

Ranger tipped his head and listened for the hum of his first aid kit. Was his work done yet?

All he heard was more men talking.

"Hey, Big Walt!" someone called.

Walt looked up and waved at some men unloading two nearby jeeps that had stopped side by side in the sand. "Go on, dog." Walt patted Ranger and pointed up ahead. "I'll be right there." He turned and headed for the jeeps.

Ranger walked on to the sheltered spot to wait. The shallow ditch was piled with soldiers' things now — packs and canteens and broken radios. Ranger poked around until he found his first aid kit where Walt had tucked it before. It was half buried in smooth stones that must have fallen on top of it in the chaos. Ranger pawed the pebbles aside and nuzzled the old metal box.

Still quiet.

Then an explosion louder than any of the others split the air. Ranger yelped. Men shouted and scrambled out of the ditch. Ranger followed them onto the sand.

The air was full of thick black smoke. And one of the jeeps was on fire.

Where was Walt?

## Chapter 12

# INTO THE FLAMES

Ranger raced toward the flames. He felt the heat of the fire on his face. Smoke burned his nose and stung his eyes. But Walt was somewhere in the middle of the chaos. Ranger had to find him.

Men ran everywhere. Others lay still on the beach near the burning jeep.

The fire popped and crackled. Where was Walt?

Ranger raced around the burning jeep.

*There!*

Walt lay crumpled in the sand, not far from the jeep's rear tires.

Ranger ran up to him and barked. He pawed at Walt's shoulder.

The fire was growing hotter by the second. Ranger's skin prickled under his fur. He had to get Walt away from here!

Ranger barked again. He nuzzled Walt's ear and licked his face.

Finally, Walt moved his head. He scrunched up his face, opened his eyes, and blinked into the smoky sky. Then he put a hand on Ranger's back and lifted himself up on his elbows. When he saw the jeep engulfed in flames, his eyes grew wide, and he pushed himself up to stand.

Ranger barked again. He jumped up on Walt and tried to push him toward the sheltered area with the stones.

Walt stumbled backward. His left leg

burned as if it were on fire. Walt reached down, and his hand came back covered in blood. The heat burned his eyes. He was choking on smoke. But other men had fallen when the German shell landed. Two of them still lay sprawled in the sand, far too close to the burning jeep. They needed help.

Walt limped over, grabbed one of the men under his arms, and tried to pull him to safety. But the man was twice Walt's size. Walt leaned back with all of his weight just to drag him a few inches. Then Walt's leg collapsed underneath him, and they both fell to the sand.

While Walt struggled to stand, Ranger raced to the other man. He pawed at the soldier's belly and licked his face. The man stirred but didn't open his eyes.

Walt braced his feet and lifted the man's torso again. But his injured leg was too shaky. He fell back just as a loud pop came from the flames. Walt looked up. The fire had spread to the second jeep. And for the first time, Walt noticed what the men had been about to unload.

Boxes of ammunition.

Cans of gasoline.

If the flames reached them, the whole jeep would explode! And anyone nearby . . .

Walt ignored the pain in his leg. He scrambled to his feet, wrapped his arms around the fallen soldier's chest, and pulled as hard as he could. He managed to drag the man back a foot or so in the sand.

The fire crackled and hissed through the front part of the second jeep, inching its way toward the explosive cargo.

Walt's face burned with heat from the fire. He braced himself and pulled again. The man slid another few inches. They weren't moving fast enough or far enough. Walt wanted to scream, but his throat burned. The fire and smoke had stolen away his voice.

How long before the whole jeep blew up around them?

Walt stared at the stacked-up gasoline cans and ammo boxes as if he could keep the fire away with his eyes. He knew that was impossible.

But there was something he could do. It might get him killed. Or it might save them all. It was a chance he had to take.

Walt sucked in a deep gulp of smoky air. Then he raced toward the burning jeep.

The fire crackled with heat that threatened to burn away Walt's uniform, but there was no time to stop and think. He had one chance.

Walt pointed to the wounded soldiers. "Stay with them!" he shouted at Ranger.

Walt staggered up to the jeep. He squeezed

his eyes shut against the heat and smoke and grabbed two of the gas cans in his arms. He lugged them away toward the water and set them down in the sand.

Then he started back toward the jeep.

Again and again, Walt plunged into the smoke and flames. Two other men rushed in to help, and together, they hauled away the rest of the gasoline and ammunition. Walt set a box of hand grenades carefully onto the wet sand and collapsed beside it, clutching the back of his leg.

Ranger raced to Walt's side and nuzzled his shoulder. Walt clenched his teeth and sat up. He put a hand on Ranger's back and stood, leaning hard against him. Together, they made their way back to the sheltered area.

Walt sank down and let out a long breath.

"You okay, Big Walt?" one of the other soldiers called out.

Walt grimaced. "Got hit with shrapnel. I need to get this bandaged, and then —"

Another soldier interrupted him. "What in the devil is a kid doing down here?"

"What?" Walt winced at the pain in his leg as he stood. He stared out over the sand and rocks. "Oh no."

Leo had left the concrete pillbox. He was walking toward them, lugging the cat under one arm. Just ahead of him was the deadly stretch of beach Walt had crossed with Ranger.

Leo was headed straight for the land mines.

## Chapter 13

## NOT ANOTHER STEP!

"No!" Walt shouted up the beach. "Go back!"

But the wind and waves swallowed his words. The boy kept coming.

Walt looked down at the golden retriever who had led him over the treacherous stretch of sand. It was a long shot. But this shaggy dog was the kid's only hope. He snapped his fingers at Ranger. "Hey! Dog!" He pointed out over the beach toward Leo. "Go get him! Help him! Okay? Go on!" He patted Ranger's backside and pointed again.

Ranger started out over the rocky beach.

"Careful!" Walt shouted.

Ranger barked, and the boy looked up. But he didn't stop walking. He was close to the part of the beach with the danger smell.

Ranger barked again. Leo stopped walking and looked up.

"Wait!" Walt was still shouting from the shingle. "Stop! Wait!"

Ranger wanted to run to help Leo. But he had to go slowly, letting his nose lead him over the sand. Twice, he caught the sharp, earthy danger smell and circled around that spot on the sand. Finally, he reached Leo.

Leo squatted down and gave Ranger a scratch behind his ear with the hand that wasn't holding the cat.

"It's okay, dog," Leo said. "The fighting's mostly over. The jeep fire's burning out. It's safe. I'm just going to make sure Walt is all right." He started forward, but Ranger stepped in front of him.

"What is it, dog?" Leo asked, trying to move around Ranger.

Ranger pawed at Leo's leg and moved to block him again.

"Go on, then." Leo waited, and Ranger started forward through the sand and weeds. When he smelled the danger smell, he stopped and sat down.

"Come on, dog." Leo urged Ranger on.

Ranger stayed put. Walt had known to circle around the chemical smell. Why didn't Leo understand? Ranger barked. Then he pawed at Leo, nudging him away from the strange smell. He barked again and started around that area of sand.

"You want me to follow you?" Leo said. "Okay."

Ranger led him on a winding path through the mines. Once the danger was behind them, he started trotting toward the sheltered area where the soldiers were resting.

Walt had harsh words for Leo when they arrived. "I told you to stay put!"

"It seemed safe. I —"

"Safe?" Walt shook his head. "You just walked through an active minefield, kid. This time, you need to listen and stay here. We need to get the balloons up by dark, before the German planes come back. Then we'll get you home."

Leo swallowed hard and nodded. He looked back up the beach and a shiver ran down his spine. Leo had seen the fallen men on the sand up there. He figured they'd been shot when the battle first started. But no. They'd been killed by exploding mines. Mines that could have killed him, too.

Leo looked down at Ranger. "You saved me, didn't you?" he whispered. Still holding the cat under one arm, he sank to his knees and wrapped the other around Ranger's neck. "Thank you, dog."

Ranger leaned into Leo's hug until the cat took a swipe at him. Then he pulled away and looked around. The soldiers were all reloading guns or eating or treating one another's injuries. One man had pulled out a soggy bandage to wrap Walt's leg wound.

"Sorry, this is the best I've got," the soldier said. "My whole pack got wet when we landed."

"I can help, now that I'm here," Leo said quietly.

Ranger wandered away. He poked around the shingle until he found his first aid kit. There was no humming. It sat quietly, nestled in the pebbles.

Ranger had arrived in the middle of a fierce

battle. He'd helped Walt save the soldiers from the waves. He'd found Leo in the fallen-down farmhouse. He'd roused Walt to save him from the burning jeep and led both of them safely through the minefield. When would he get to go home? Ranger pawed at the old metal box, but it still didn't make a sound.

"Hey, wait. That looks dry," one of the soldiers said. He reached over, picked up Ranger's first aid kit, and opened it. "Here we go." He pulled out some bandages.

Leo poured clean water over Walt's leg wound. Then he helped the soldier wrap it in a clean, dry bandage.

"You going to be a doctor one day?" Walt asked.

Leo shook his head. "I want to be a teacher like my father," he said. "But my grandmother is a nurse. She taught all of us a bit of medicine. Papa said that was good. We have to care

for one another since no one else does." He looked at Walt and whispered, "My family is Jewish. They treat us like we're not even people. It's been . . ." He swallowed hard and shook his head. "Sorry. You wouldn't understand."

Walt put a hand on the boy's shoulder. "I understand more than you think," he said quietly. "In America, people like me know how it feels to be looked at like you're worth less than everyone else. That's why we're here," he added. "Part of it anyway. To prove we can do a job just as good as anybody. Twice as good. Even in the army, they keep us separate, like we can't do the same work." He looked out over the beach. "But here we are, aren't we? Pretty soon, we'll get our balloons in the sky to keep the German planes away tonight. After that, we'll follow whatever orders come next. Then maybe when we get home . . ." He didn't finish.

"You good now, Big Walt?" one of the other soldiers called over.

"Let's go." Walt pushed himself up and looked down at Leo. "You stay here this time. I mean it."

"I will," Leo said.

Walt nodded. "All right, then. Time to raise some balloons."

## Chapter 14

# RAISE THE BALLOONS

The light was already fading when Walt and the other men from his battalion began moving balloons into place. Walt's leg wound burned, but there was no time to rest. German planes would arrive with the darkness, carrying bombs meant to take out the Allied forces hunkered down on the beaches and along the ridge. It was a race against time, and the wind wasn't helping.

Walt and two other men had just begun unwinding the cable to raise the first balloon when a gust whipped over the beach. The balloon's mooring lines were weighted down with sandbags, but it wasn't enough.

"Hold the cables!" Walt called. Every man grabbed a line and held on. The balloon bucked in the wind, a wild horse trying to break free. "Keep the nose in the air or we'll lose it!"

A mooring line snapped loose from a heap of sandbags.

"Watch out!" someone shouted.

Ranger barked.

Walt raised his hands to shield his face. The cable whipped against him, but he grabbed at it. The steel line slid through his gloves, but at the last second, he got a grip on it and planted his feet in the sand. "Hold on!" he shouted to the other men.

The wind roared over the waves. It gave the balloon one last great tug that nearly lifted Walt off his feet. But then it let up for a moment, and that was all it took for the men to secure the lines again.

"We can't wait any longer," one of the soldiers said, looking at the darkening sky. "We have to get it up. Ready?"

"Ready!" Walt secured his line to a sandbag and hurried to the winch that controlled the balloon's main cable. Slowly, bit by bit, he let out the line that allowed the balloon to rise. The other men guided their mooring lines until the big metallic balloon floated like a shadow two thousand feet over the beach.

Walt let out a long breath. The balloons' defense wasn't perfect, but any German pilot who dared to fly low over their troops would risk having his plane brought down by a wing snagged in the cables.

This first balloon was only a start.

"Let's go! We have to keep moving!" Walt shouted. He worked alongside the other men

from the 320th all night long. Twice, he heard the buzz of a German plane. Twice, the pilots approached and suddenly veered away. Had the balloons scared them off?

There was no time to celebrate. Too much work still had to be done.

Ranger stayed near Walt and the other soldiers for a while, but they kept tripping over him. Finally, he left and went to sit with Leo in the dark.

The cat was already curled up, asleep, but Leo was sitting, looking out at the teams of men working all over the beach. "They really came," he whispered. "Mémère promised they would. I so wanted to believe, but I wondered. Two years is such a long time to wait." Leo yawned and patted Ranger on the head.

Ranger didn't know what Leo was saying, but he understood that sometimes people just needed to talk. They didn't expect you to

understand or answer. Luke did that sometimes, especially when he was sad or scared.
When Leo finally curled up and closed his
eyes, Ranger snuggled close beside him. But
he stayed awake all night long, watching the
men work on the beach, waiting for them to
finish.

Maybe then, Ranger's work here would be
done, too.

## Chapter 15

# SAYING GOOD-BYE

When the sun woke Leo at dawn, a dozen balloons hung in a curtain over the beach. Walt and the other men had already loaded up their things.

"Is it time to go?" Leo asked. He stood and brushed the wet sand from his trousers. "Do you want me to carry something?"

"Sure. Good to have this, just in case." Walt handed Ranger's first aid kit to Leo.

"Are you all going to stay in our village?" Leo asked.

Walt shook his head. "Not for long. My

battalion will be here awhile manning the balloons to protect the beach while they bring in more trucks and supplies. After that . . . we'll go wherever we're needed next." He let out a long, tired sigh. "Come on. Let's get moving."

Leo scooped up his cat and fell into line with the soldiers. Ranger walked between him and Walt. They made a long, wide circle around the dangerous area with the mines. They climbed over the ridge and along the plateau.

Soon, Leo spotted his village in the early morning light. His eyes landed on the heap of wood and stone where the Blancs' farmhouse used to be. It was completely destroyed. But when they got closer, Leo's heart lifted with hope. Mr. Blanc and the boys were walking toward the barn. They'd survived the night in the ditch!

Leo wanted to run ahead to meet them but

thought he should stay with Walt and the other men, so he kept marching. The village was full of Allied soldiers. Even with all the damage from Allied bombs in the days before the invasion, people smiled and waved at them. Women brought out jugs of cider. Children chased after the American jeeps with bouquets of flowers.

The Blancs were near the barn door, talking with some American servicemen when Leo and the others arrived. Belle squirmed in Leo's arms, and he put her down so she could go inside. Mr. Blanc looked up. "Henri!" he called.

Leo dropped the first aid kit in the weeds and ran into the farmer's arms.

Mr. Blanc turned to Walt and the other men. "Thank you. We never gave up hope. We knew you'd come." Then he looked down at Ranger. "Is this an Allied dog?"

"I guess so," Leo said. He looked at Walt.

Walt nodded, though he still didn't know where the dog had come from. He looked back over his shoulder. The other men in his battalion were already moving on. "I should go. We have work to do. But I wish you all well." He started off toward the other men.

"Wait!" Leo called out. He ran to Walt and took his hand. "Thank you. I . . . I just wish you could stay."

"It's all right." Walt knelt down. "You'll be safe now."

"But what if the Germans come back?" Leo said in a small voice.

"They won't," Walt said. "We'll make sure. Look." He pointed to the monument down the road. During the occupation, German soldiers had taken down the French flag in the village square. Today, three of the local men were raising it again, with Allied soldiers looking on. Seeing the red, white, and blue of his country's flag made Leo feel a little better.

Mr. Blanc stepped up to his side. "Soon, the Allies will liberate Paris," he said, "and your grandmother will come for you."

"And the rest of my family?" Leo said.

"I hope so." Mr. Blanc swallowed hard and looked away. "I will never stop hoping."

"Neither will I," Leo said. He turned back to Walt. "Thank you. Again." He knelt down. "And thank you, too, dog. I'll never forget you." He gave Ranger a tight hug.

Ranger nuzzled Leo's shoulder. The boy smelled like sand and salt and sweat. Also, cat.

Ranger sneezed. Leo gave him one last pat, waved good-bye to Walt, and headed off to help the Blancs find the rest of their animals.

"Take care," Walt said, and started walking away.

Ranger stood by the barn. He watched Leo, hurrying down the road to catch up to Mr. Blanc. Leo was safe now.

Ranger looked at Walt, falling into line with the other soldiers. There was no more gunfire today. The smoke was clearing. The air was crisp and quiet.

Except for a quiet hum coming from the weeds.

Walt looked back over his shoulder. "You coming, dog?"

Ranger sat down. He wasn't. The humming was already getting louder. It was time to go home.

Walt jogged back to Ranger. "You staying here? All right." Walt squatted down and gave Ranger's neck a good scratch. When he did, a folded-up paper fell from his jacket pocket. It was soggy and torn, but Walt could still make out the words printed on it. It was his order from General Eisenhower. "The eyes of the world are upon you . . ."

Walt looked down at Ranger. "You carried out your duty as well as any of us, dog. Here . . ." He folded up the soggy paper and tucked it under Ranger's collar. "You remember Big Walt, all right?" He gave Ranger one more scratch and ran to catch up with the rest of the soldiers.

Ranger turned and poked through the weeds until he found his first aid kit. It was humming loudly now.

Ranger nuzzled the strap over his neck. The old metal box grew warm at his throat. Light spilled from the cracks. The humming grew louder and louder. The light became brighter and brighter. Soon, Ranger couldn't see the soldiers or the fallen-down farmhouse or the village anymore. He felt as if he were being squeezed through a hole in the sky. He closed his eyes until the humming finally stopped.

When he opened them, Luke was walking into the mudroom with a dish of cold water.

## Chapter 16

# COMING HOME

"Here you go, Ranger!" Luke said. "No wonder you're thirsty. That was some day at the beach, huh?"

Ranger lowered his head and let the first aid kit fall to his dog bed. He nuzzled Luke's hand and dipped his head for a good, long drink of water. While he drank, Luke stroked the fur on his back.

"You've still got some sand in your fur," he said. "We'll have to get out the dog brush later. Or you could have a bath." He patted Ranger's head and then said, "Hey . . . what's this?"

Luke pulled out the scrap of paper and unfolded it. "'You are about to embark upon the Great Crusade, toward which we have striven these many months,'" he read. "'The eyes of the world are upon you. The hopes and prayers of liberty-loving people everywhere march with you . . .' It's by General Eisenhower. Wasn't he a World War Two guy?" Luke looked down at Ranger. "Where'd you get this? You didn't chew up my social studies textbook, did you?" Luke stood and picked up his school bag from the mudroom bench. He poked through it and pulled out a book. It was fine. "Huh," Luke said, looking down at the paper.

Ranger looked up at Luke. He pawed at Luke's hand, and Luke laughed. "Okay . . . I'm sorry I accused you of chewing up my school stuff. Here . . ." He dropped the slip of paper onto Ranger's dog bed. "Don't know where you found that, but it's all yours."

"Luke!" Sadie called from the porch. "Mom wants you to come help put away the beach toys!"

When Luke was gone, Ranger took another good, cold drink from his water dish. It really had been quite a day at the beach.

Then he walked over to his dog bed. Walt's damp folded-up paper was there. Ranger picked it up in his teeth, careful not to drool on it. It was already pretty soggy. He nuzzled his blanket aside to reveal his other treasures . . . the quilt square from the lonely boy named Sam, the funny leaf from Marcus, the broken metal brooch from Helga, the little yellow feather from Lily, and a bigger brown-and-white-striped one from a girl named Sarah. Ranger dropped Walt's paper onto the pile and pawed at his blanket until everything was tucked safely away.

The first aid kit rested in the corner of

Ranger's dog bed. It was quiet now, and that was good. Somehow, Ranger knew that even though Walt and Leo had more battles and sad days ahead, they would be safe. And when it was all over, they'd both get to go home, too.

Ranger went outside and flopped down on the front porch. He'd never forget the two brave young men he'd met by that faraway ocean. He'd miss Leo's quiet hand on his back and Walt's friendly neck scratches. But he was so, so happy to be home.

## AUTHOR'S NOTE

Walt and Leo are both fictional characters, but their stories are based on the experiences of real people who lived through the dark days of World War II in Europe and the liberation of France that began with the Allied invasion of Normandy on June 6, 1944.

Like Leo, many Jewish children from Paris were brought to hide with families in the countryside when Nazi soldiers and the French police who cooperated with them began rounding up Jewish people and sending them to concentration camps. These weren't really camps. They were prisons where Jewish people were forced to work under horrific conditions. They were abused, and millions were killed. The persecution and murder of Jewish people by Nazis and their collaborators was carried out across Nazi-occupied Europe and is now known as the Holocaust. In the early days of the occupation, the Nazis targeted innocent Jewish people based only on who they were, what they looked like, and what they believed. Nazis blamed

Jewish people for society's problems, forced them to register with the government, and required them to wear gold stars to identify themselves wherever they went.

The persecution got worse and worse. On November 9–10, 1938, Nazis attacked Jewish people throughout Germany. The Nazis burned synagogues, vandalized homes and businesses, and murdered dozens of Jewish people. This wave of violence is known as Kristallnacht, or the Night of Broken Glass. Many historians mark this night as the beginning of the Holocaust.

In the years that followed, more and more Jewish people were taken from their homes and businesses throughout Nazi-occupied Europe. In July 1942, French police rounded up around 13,000 French Jews and brought them to the Vélodrome d'Hiver, a Paris cycling stadium. Like Leo's parents and sister, thousands were held for days with little food or water before being sent to a concentration camp. The Shoah Memorial in Paris has a display that bears witness to these awful days. It includes the only known photograph of what's now known as the Vel' d'Hiv roundup, showing transport trucks lined up outside the Paris stadium.

The memorial's display also includes a letter from a French girl whose family was ripped from their homes on the morning of July 16. Leo's story is partly based on her recollections. *Good-bye for Always: The Triumph of the Innocents* includes another first-person account of the Vel' d'Hiv roundup. In it, Cecile Kaufer and Joe Allen tell the story of Cecile's childhood in Nazi-occupied France. Leo's escape from the roundup via his mother's trip to the hospital was inspired by Cecile's real-life story.

The Vélodrome d'Hiver stadium is gone now, replaced by modern buildings. But nearby, along the banks of the Seine not far from the Eiffel Tower, is a memorial.

More than six million Jewish people were killed during the Holocaust. I understand that at the end of this story, many readers will wonder if Leo is ever reunited with his family. While there are a handful of stories

from this time period with happy endings, historical documents tell us that most Jewish families separated during the roundups never saw their loved ones again. In Leo's case, I've left that question for readers to decide.

In researching this book, I spent a week in France, exploring museums that interpret this dark time period in European history. I'm most appreciative of the wonderful staffs at the Memorial of Caen Museum in Normandy as well as the Army Museum at Les Invalides and the Shoah Memorial in Paris. I also spent several days on the beaches where the Allied invasion began. D-Day guide and scholar Claire Lesourd was an invaluable resource who helped me to trace the steps of the men of the 320th and translated during interviews. (And thanks to Gwen Queguiner, who helped out later by translating sections of the interview that went by too quickly to transcribe on the spot.) I'm also most grateful to Jeannette Legallois, who invited my family to sit at her kitchen table while she shared her memories of the day Allied soldiers came to liberate her town.

Many of Leo's stories of life at the farmhouse are based on Jeannette's recollections. She was fifteen years old in 1944 and shared how difficult her family's life was under the

German occupation. She used to play in the garden while her father listened to the family's secret crystal radio, ready to warn him if German soldiers approached. She still remembers the sound of the soldiers' boots on the cobblestones. The Germans demanded five liters of milk each day, and her brother was so angry about this that he really did stick his finger in the milk "to put germs in it." As farmers, Jeannette's family had more food than most during the shortages, so she'd sneak meat in her schoolbag to share with people who were hungry.

One of her neighbors' houses was destroyed by Allied bombs in the days leading up to the invasion. So while her village celebrated the arrival of the Allies, the day was also marked by sadness because so many people had been hurt or killed, and so many buildings had been destroyed. She remembers the never-ending line of American jeeps driving through her village and how the children chased the vehicles with bouquets of flowers, so excited they'd forget to watch for traffic.

Now Jeannette's family runs a charming farm market not far from her old village. Photographs displayed on the buildings tell the story of the town's liberation from the Nazis, including the return of the French flag.

Today, the nearby beaches are peaceful. But they are still full of German bunkers and machine gun nests, reminders of that morning in 1944.

The concrete building near the ridge where Leo finds Walt is based on a real German pillbox that still stands near the bluff that leads to the seaside village of Saint-Laurent-sur-Mer. One of the balloons of the 320th can be seen flying over this spot in one of the historical photos displayed at the site.

Soldat américain et civils aux
Monument aux morts
à SAINT-LAURENT-SUR-MER
GI's with french civilians at the
memorial in SAINT-LAURENT-SUR-MER
(8)

Like Leo, Walt Burrell is a fictional character, but he was inspired by the real heroes of the 320th Barrage Balloon Battalion. Their mission was to raise balloons over the beach to protect Allied soldiers from German bombers. While more than two thousand

African-American soldiers participated in the Allied invasion, most were part of support units that transported supplies or took care of vehicles. The 320th was the only African-American combat unit to come ashore on D-Day.

World War II happened before the civil rights movement, when Americans protested to end the practice of segregating people based on race. At the time of the Normandy invasion, the military was still completely segregated. African-American men like Walt were allowed to serve their country and die in battle, but they weren't allowed to eat in the same mess halls or serve in the same units as white soldiers. The 621 members of the 320th who landed on Omaha Beach suffered heavy casualties. Three of them are buried in the American Cemetery at Omaha Beach — James McLean, Brooks Stith, and Henry J. Harris.

You won't see members of the 320th Barrage Balloon Battalion portrayed in popular D-Day movies. Their country largely ignored them until recently. But in 2009, William Dabney, the only living member of the 320th officials could track down, returned to Omaha Beach and joined President Barack Obama to commemorate the sixty-fifth anniversary of D-Day. The *New York Times* published

an article about Dabney's trip, and his mission sixty-five years earlier: http://www.nytimes.com/2009/06/06/world/europe/06iht-troops.html.

While Walt's story is made up, it was inspired by the real-life heroics of Dabney and another member of the 320th named Waverly Woodson. Linda Hervieux's excellent book *Forgotten: The Untold Story of D-Day's Black Heroes, at Home and at War* gives a detailed account of the lives of Dabney, Woodson, and other men of the 320th and was a wonderful resource as well.

I'm also grateful to the family of Waverly Woodson for sharing documents that tell his story online and emailing me about their ongoing efforts to see him honored for his service.

At the time of World War II, African-American soldiers weren't just discriminated against when it came to separate housing and mess halls. They were also ignored when it came to America's highest military honors. After World War II, the United States awarded

433 Medals of Honor, its highest honor. None of them went to African-American men. It wasn't until 1995 that the country took another look at that injustice, and an independent army investigation found that racism was to blame. In 1997, President Bill Clinton awarded the Medal of Honor to seven African American veterans of World War II. Only one of them, Vernon Baker, was still alive to receive the honor himself.

Waverly Woodson was a medic with the 320th. He was wounded on D-Day but went on to rescue several other men, pulling soldiers from the water, resuscitating them, and treating the wounded until he finally collapsed himself. Based on his heroic efforts, Woodson was recommended for a Medal of Honor.

Woodson's family has shared an extensive collection of documents detailing his service, including an Office of War Information memo to the White House about Woodson's Medal of Honor recommendation. The memo explains, "This is a big enough award so that the President can give it personally, as he has in the case of some white boys."

Woodson never received his Medal of Honor. He was awarded a Purple Heart, for soldiers injured or killed in service, and a Bronze Star, the country's fourth-highest honor, instead. What happened? His family has asked, but they've never gotten answers.

Waverly Woodson died in 2005, but his widow and other family members are still fighting for the honor they believe he deserves. They've launched a petition, requesting that Woodson finally be awarded the Medal of Honor for which he was recommended so long ago.

# FURTHER READING

Waverly Woodson's family has shared all of the documents they've submitted in their request for him to receive the Medal of Honor. The collection includes Woodson's own recollections of D-Day as well as a hand-written letter to his dad: http://stateside.digitalnewsroom.org/wp-content/uploads/2015/11/Woodson-Waverly-Enclosed-Docs-Sent-to-Army-11.5.15.-No-PR.pdf

Linda Hervieux, the author of *Forgotten: The Untold Story of D-Day's Black Heroes, at Home and at War*, has a wonderful website with photographs and information about real-life members of the 320th Barrage Balloon Battalion, including Waverly Woodson. You can read more and learn how to support his family's petition here: http://www.lindahervieux.com/the-320th-blog/2015/9/3/waverly-b-woodson-jr. (Be sure to get a parent or guardian's permission before sharing any information online.)

This *Time* magazine article takes a closer look at why African American soldiers didn't receive Medals of Honor after World War II and what's being done about it now: http://time.com/4064931/wwii-african-american-medal-of-honor-reunited/

The United States Holocaust Memorial Museum has a comprehensive list of recommended titles that address this period in history, with age range suggestions for each: https://www.ushmm.org/research/research-in-collections/search-the-collections/bibliography/childrens-books

Here are some additional books for readers who would like to learn more about the Holocaust, segregation in the United States, the Battle of Normandy, and working dogs.

*The Butterfly* by Patricia Polacco (Penguin Books, 2000)

*Freedom on the Menu: The Greensboro Sit-Ins* by Carol Boston Weatherford, illustrated by Jerome Lagarrigue (Penguin Books, 2007)

*The Greatest Skating Race: A World War II Story from the Netherlands* by Louise Borden, illustrated by Niki Daly (Simon & Schuster, 2004)

*I Survived the Nazi Invasion, 1944* by Lauren Tarshis (Scholastic, 2014)

*Rosa* by Nikki Giovanni, illustrated by Bryan Collier (Macmillan, 2005)

*The Secret Seder* by Doreen Rappaport, illustrated by Emily Arnold McCully (Hyperion, 2005)

*Sniffer Dogs: How Dogs (and Their Noses) Save the World* by Nancy Castaldo (Houghton Mifflin Harcourt, 2014)

*Terrible Things: An Allegory of the Holocaust* by Eve Bunting, illustrated by Stephen Gammell (Harper & Row, 1980)

*What Was D-Day?* by Patricia Brennan Demuth, illustrated by David Grayson Kenyon (Grosset & Dunlap, 2015)

*Wind Flyers* by Angela Johnson, illustrated by Loren Long (Simon & Schuster, 2007)

*You Can Fly: The Tuskegee Airmen* by Carole Boston Weatherford, illustrated by Jeffery Boston Weatherford (Simon & Schuster, 2016)

# SOURCES

Abrami, Leo Michel. *Evading the Nazis: The Story of a Hidden Child in Normandy*. Denver, CO: Outskirts Press, 2009.

Ambrose, Stephen E. *D-Day: June 6, 1944: The Battle for the Normandy Beaches*. New York: Simon & Schuster, 1994.

American Rescue Dog Association. *Search and Rescue Dogs: Training the K-9 Hero*. Hoboken, NJ: Wiley Publishing, 2002.

Bulanda, Susan. *Ready! Training the Search and Rescue Dog*. Freehold, NJ: Kennel Club Books, 2010.

Hammond, Shirley M. *Training the Disaster Search Dog*. Wenatchee, WA: Dogwise Publishing, 2006.

Hervieux, Linda. *Forgotten: The Untold Story of D-Day's Black Heroes, at Home and at War*. New York: HarperCollins, 2015.

Kaufer, Cecile, and Joe Allen. *Good-bye for Always: The Triumph of the Innocents*. Tomkins Cove, NY: Hudson Cove Publishing, 1997.

Quellien, Jean. *Normandy 44*. Bayeux, France: OREP Editions, 2011.

# ABOUT THE AUTHOR

**Kate Messner** is the author of *The Seventh Wish*; *All the Answers*; *The Brilliant Fall of Gianna Z.*, recipient of the E. B. White Read Aloud Award for Older Readers; *Capture the Flag*, a Crystal Kite Award winner; *Over and Under the Snow*, a *New York Times* Notable Children's Book; and the Ranger in Time and Marty McGuire chapter book series. A former middle-school English teacher, Kate lives on Lake Champlain with her family and loves reading, walking in the woods, and traveling. Visit her online at www.katemessner.com.

Ranger arrives in New Orleans and meets Clare Porter, who is searching for her grandmother as Hurricane Katrina approaches. Ranger helps Clare find Nana and takes shelter with them at their home in the Lower Ninth Ward, waiting for Clare's father to return. But there's no sign of him as hours pass and the weather gets worse. Can Ranger lead Clare and Nana through the flooded city to safety? Keep reading for a sneak peek!

When Clare Porter's dad dropped her off to volunteer at the SPCA on Saturday morning, the neighborhood hummed with activity. Traffic helicopters buzzed overhead. Neighbors hammered plywood over windows, getting ready for the storm. Two big trucks were parked outside the animal shelter.

"What's going on?" Clare asked James, one of the older volunteers.

"We're moving the animals to Houston," James told her. "Katrina is a Category Three hurricane now. Procedure says we have to evacuate the shelter. I'm working on ID collars. We also need to take photos of all the dogs and cats before they're loaded onto the truck." He handed Clare a camera, and she set to work.

"Smile, Bugsy!" she told a grumpy bulldog mix. She'd met him on her first day volunteering at the shelter last fall, right after she'd turned eleven.

"Your family leaving?" James asked Clare as he fastened a collar on a squirmy orange cat.

"Mom and my little brothers have been visiting Aunt Celeste in Houston. They're going to stay a few extra days," Clare said. "Daddy and I are staying here with my grandmother to ride out the storm unless it gets real bad."

James raised his eyebrows. "Already starting to look like a big one."

"We'll be careful." Clare looked at the pale, quiet sky. It was hard to imagine a monster hurricane just two days away. Aside from getting their houses ready, most of her neighbors in the Lower Ninth Ward of New Orleans were going about their business. Dad had taken Nana to basketball practice right after he'd dropped Clare off to work at the shelter. Nana used to be one of the star players on the Silver Slammers, her basketball team for women sixty years and older. But Nana was eighty now, and last year, she started forgetting things. She couldn't remember the rules. She couldn't really play in games anymore, but she still went to practice to shoot baskets. Practice had gone on today, just like always.

But by the time Clare's father picked her up, more and more neighbors were packing their cars.

"We've got time," Dad said. He scooped some of Nana's red beans and rice into a bowl for dinner and limped over to the table. His knee still bothered him from when he got hurt in the Army a long time ago.

"I still think the storm will turn," Dad said. "We'll wait and see."

Later, after she was in bed, Clare heard him on the phone with her mother. "I know. But evacuation would be mandatory if they thought the storm was going to hit that hard . . . Okay . . . Love you, too."

On Sunday morning, Clare woke to the sound of the news on TV.

"Devastating damage is expected, rivaling the intensity of Hurricane Camille of 1969 . . ."

Clare shivered. Dad had told her stories about Camille. Back then the flooding was so bad that he and Grandpa had to break out of their attic with an axe and wait on the roof to be rescued.

"Clare?" Dad called. Clare found him in the kitchen at the front of their long, skinny house, filling a cooler. "The mayor just ordered a mandatory evacuation. We're leaving. Pack clothes for a week," he told her.

"A week?!"

"Just in case," Dad said. "Storm's getting stronger. I'm going to put gas in the car. Mrs. Jackson next door is coming with us, too."

"Mrs. Jackson? How come?" Clare asked.

"She doesn't have family here," Dad said. "So we need to look out for her. No one gets left behind on my watch."

Clare nodded. She hadn't been born yet when her father served in the Army during Operation Desert Storm, but she knew the story of how he got hurt. He'd run out from behind a jeep to rescue another soldier who had fallen during a firefight. Dad said he had to go, even though it was dangerous. You never leave a fallen soldier. It was an Army promise. The mission wasn't over until everyone made it out.

"We'll leave as soon as I get back," Dad said. "Keep an eye on Nana while I'm gone."

"Okay." Clare headed down the hallway. "Are you getting clothes together, Nana?" she called into her grandmother's bedroom.

"I'm staying right here," Nana said. "I have practice tonight." She held up her Silver Slammers warm-up jacket.

Clare sighed. "There won't be practice with the storm, Nana. Everyone's leaving. Pack your clothes, okay?"

Clare went to her bedroom and threw shorts and T-shirts into a backpack. She was in the middle of reading *Bud, Not Buddy* again, so she packed that, too. Then she took it back out to read as she waited for Dad. She liked all of Bud's funny rules for getting by in the world.

After a while, the wind rattled her window, and Clare looked up. It had already been half an hour. Just how far did Dad have to go for gas? Clare hoped he'd find an open station soon so they could head out.

The sky grew darker and darker. Clare turned on a light. The wind slammed a door shut somewhere. Clare looked at the clock. It was already noon. She texted her father.

*When will you be home?*

He didn't reply. So Clare turned on the radio.

"At least one-half of well-constructed homes will have roof and wall failure," an announcer said. "Water shortages will make human suffering incredible by modern standards. Once tropical storm and hurricane force winds onset, do not venture outside."

Clare closed her book. She rushed to the living room. The door was partway open, thumping back and forth on its hinges. Clare looked out. There was no sign of Dad. And the rain had already started.

# MEET RANGER

## A time–traveling golden retriever with search-and-rescue training . . . and a nose for danger!